MY
BIG Book of
Beginner Books
about ME

MY
BIG Book of

Beginner Books about ME

By

Dr. Seuss,

Dr. Seuss and Joe Mathieu,

Al Perkins and Henry Payne,

Al Perkins and Joe Mathieu,

Graham Tether and Sylvie Wickstrom

RANDOM HOUSE NEW YORK

Visit us on the Web!
Seussville.com
randomhousekids.com

Educators and librarians, for a variety of teaching tools, visit us at
RHTeachersLibrarians.com

ISBN: 978-0-307-93183-2

Library of Congress Control Number: 2011935067

MANUFACTURED IN CHINA

25

Dr. Seuss's real name was Theodor Geisel.
On books he wrote to be illustrated by others,
he used the name Theo. LeSieg,
which is Geisel spelled backward.

Contents

The Foot Book   9

The Eye Book   39

The Ear Book   69

The Nose Book   99

The Tooth Book   129

The Knee Book   171

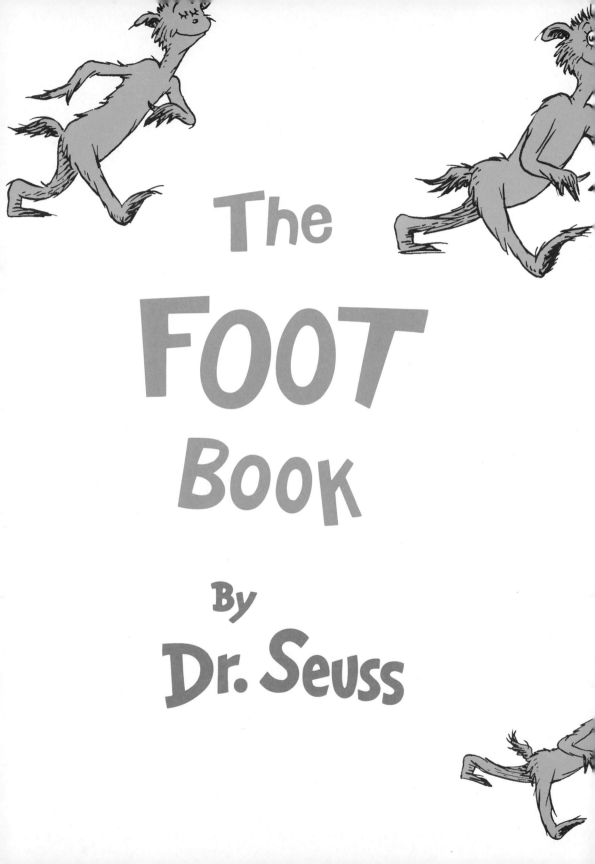

The FOOT BOOK

By Dr. Seuss

Left foot
Left foot

Right foot
Right

Feet in the morning

Feet at night

Left foot

Left foot

Left foot

Right

13

Wet foot

Dry foot

14

High foot

Low foot

Front feet

Back feet

Red feet

Black feet

Left foot   Right foot

Feet   Feet   Feet

18

How many, many
feet you meet.

Slow feet

Quick feet

Trick feet

Sick feet

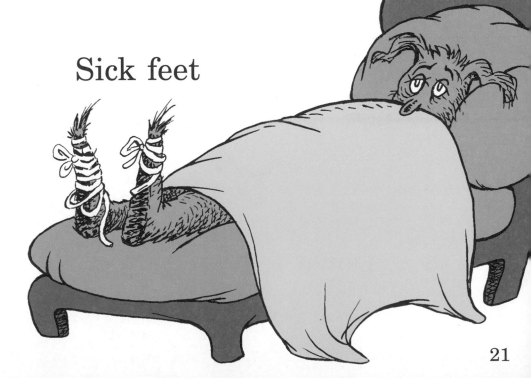

Up feet

Down feet

Here come clown feet.

Small feet

Big feet

Here come pig feet.

His feet

Her feet

Fuzzy fur feet

In the house,
and on the street,

how many, many
feet you meet.

Up in the air feet

Over a chair feet

More and more feet

Twenty-four feet

Here come
more and more............

. . . . and more feet!

Left foot.   Right foot.

Feet. Feet. Feet.

Oh, how many
feet you meet!

The EYE BOOK

By **Dr. Seuss***

***writing as**

Theo. LeSieg

Illustrated by Joe Mathieu

Eye

Eyes

My eyes
My eyes

His eyes

His eyes

Wink eye
Wink eye

Pink eye   Pink eye

My eyes see.

His eyes see.

47

I see him.

And he sees me.

Our eyes see blue.

Our eyes see red.

They see a bird.

They see a bed.

They see the sun.

They see the moon.

They see a fork

a knife

a spoon.

They see a girl.

They see a man . . .

a boy

a horse

an old tin can.

They look down holes.

They look up poles.

Our eyes see trees.

They look at clocks.

They look at bees.

They look at socks.

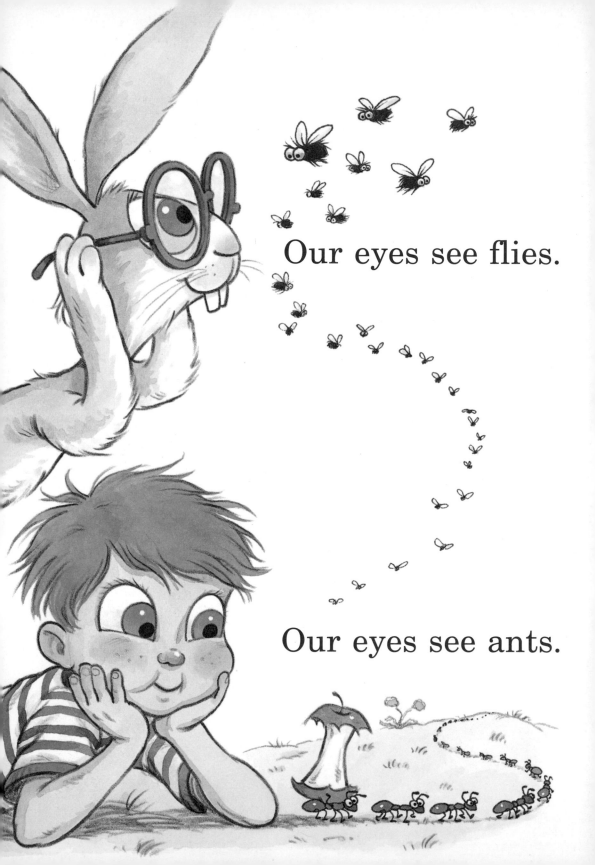

Our eyes see flies.

Our eyes see ants.

Sometimes they see
pink underpants.

Our eyes see rings.

Our eyes see strings.

They see
so many, many things!

So many things!

Like rain

and pie . . .

and dogs

and airplanes
in the sky!

And so we say,
"Hooray for eyes!
Hooray, hooray, hooray . . .

. . . for eyes!"

The EAR BOOK

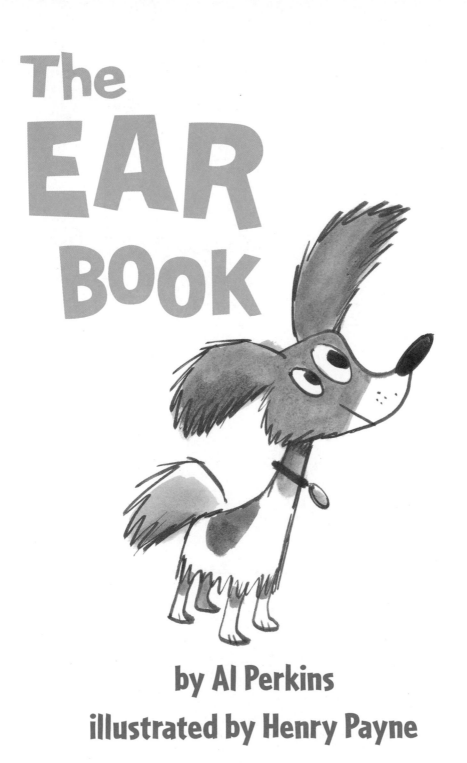

by Al Perkins

illustrated by Henry Payne

Tick

Tock

Tick

Tock

Ears

Our ears

They hear a clock.

Our ears hear water.

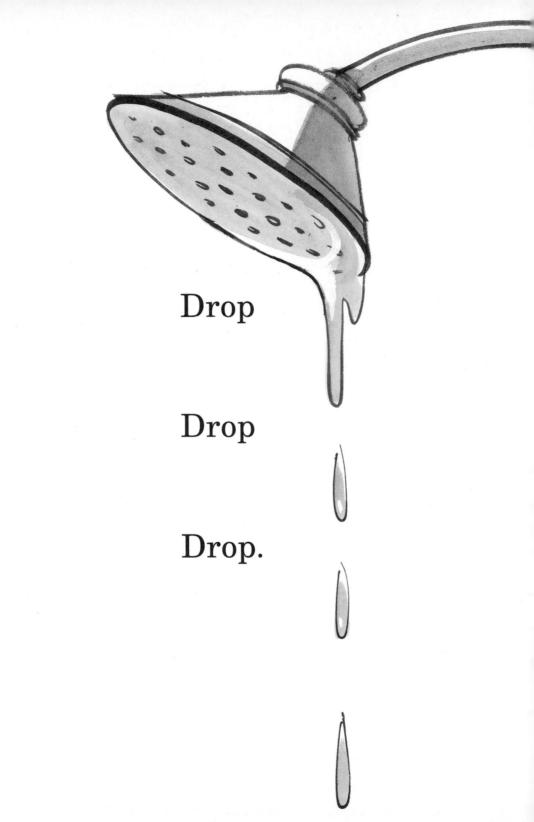

Drop

Drop

Drop.

Our ears hear popcorn.

Pop

Pop

Pop!

Ears Ears
Ears
Ears

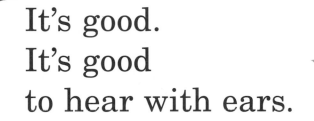

It's good.
It's good
to hear with ears.

Toot
Toot
Toot

We hear a flute.

We hear a Ding.
We hear a Dong.

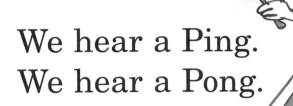

We hear a Ping.
We hear a Pong.

We hear my sister
sing a song.

We also hear
my father snore.

We hear my sister
slam the door.

Boom! Boom!
Boom! Boom!
Dum! Dum! Dum!

It's good
to hear
a drummer drum . . .

and Sister blowing
bubble gum.

We hear hands clap

and fingers snap.

We hear feet
tap
tap tap
tap tap.

We hear a plane.
We hear a train.

It's good.
It's good
to hear the rain.

Ears. Ears. Ears!
We like our ears.
It's very good
to hear
with ears.

The NOSE BOOK

By **Al Perkins**

Illustrated by **Joe Mathieu**

Everybody
grows
a nose.

I see a nose
on every face.

I see noses
every place!

A nose
between
each pair of eyes.

Noses!
Noses!
Every size.

They grow
on every
kind of head.

They come in blue . . .
. . . and pink
. . . and red.

Some are
very, very long.

Some are
very, very strong.

Everywhere a fellow goes,
he sees some
new, new kind of nose.

A nose is useful.
After all . . .
some play horns . . .

. . . and some play ball.

A nose is good
for making holes
. . . in trees

. . . and roofs

. . . and barber poles.

But sometimes
noses aren't much fun.
They sniffle.

They get burned by sun.

A nose gets punched . . .

. . . and bumped on doors

. . . and bumped on walls

. . . and bumped on floors!

Sometimes
your nose
will make you sad.
Sometimes
your nose
will make you mad.
BUT . . .

Just suppose
you had no nose!
Then you
could never
smell
a rose . . .

. . . or pie, or chicken à la king.

You'd never smell a single thing.

And one thing more.
Suppose . . . no nose . . .

Where would
all our glasses sit?
They'd all fall off!
Just THINK of it!

And that's why
everybody grows,
between his eyes,
some kind of nose!

126

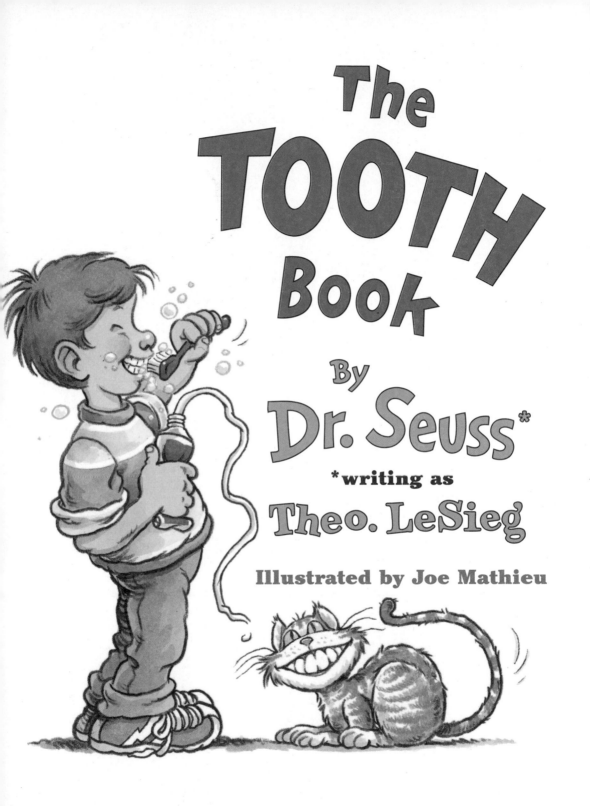

The TOOTH Book

By
Dr. Seuss*
*writing as
Theo. LeSieg

Illustrated by Joe Mathieu

Who has teeth?

Well . . .
look around
and you'll find out who.
You'll find
that red-headed uncles do.

Policemen do.
And zebras too.

And unicycle riders do.

And camels
and their drivers do!

Even little girls named Ruthie
all have teeth.
All Ruths are toothy.

Teeth!
You find them everywhere!
On mountaintops!
And in the air!

And if you care
to poke around,
you'll even find them
underground.

You'll find them
east, west, north, and south.
You'll find them
in a lion's mouth.

TEETH!
They are very much in style.

140

They must be
very much
worthwhile!

"They come in handy
when you chew,"
says Mr. Donald Driscoll Drew.

"That's why
my family
grew a few."

"They come in handy when you smile," says Smiling Sam the crocodile.

"They come in handy
in my job,"
says high trapezer
Mike McCobb.

"If I should ever
    lose a tooth,
    I'd lose my wife.
    And that's the truth."

"Teeth come in handy
when you speak,"
says news broadcaster
Quincy Queek.

"Without my teeth
I'd talk like ducks,
and only broadcast
quacks and klucks."

"You're lucky
that you have your teeth,"
says a sad, sad snail
named Simon Sneeth.

"I don't have one!
I can never smile
like Smiling Sam the crocodile."

"Clams have no teeth,"
says Pam the clam.
"I cannot eat
hot dogs
or ham."

"No teeth at all,"
    says Pam the clam.
"I cannot eat
    roast leg of lamb.
    Or peanuts! Pizzas!
    Popcorn! SPAM!
    Not even huckleberry jam!"

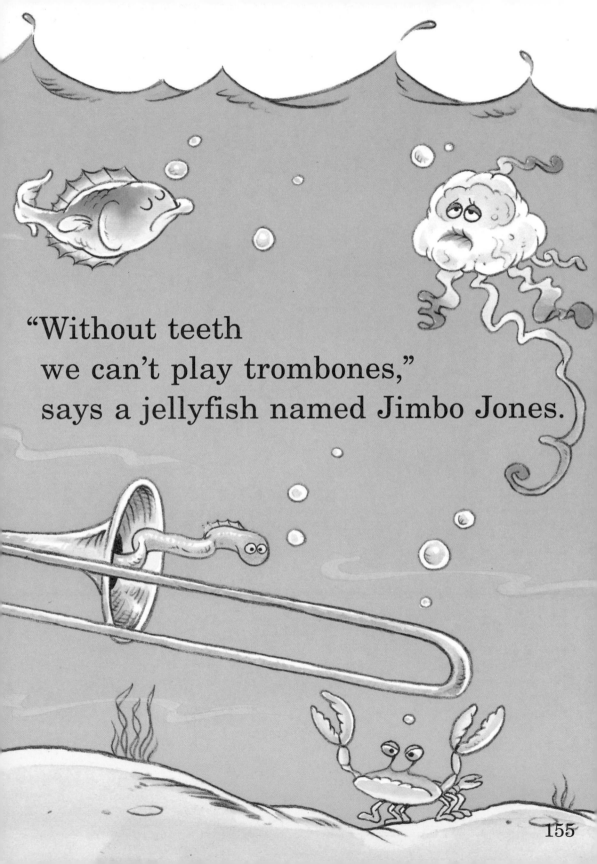

"Without teeth
we can't play trombones,"
says a jellyfish named Jimbo Jones.

"I have no teeth,"
says Hilda Hen.
"But women do.
And so do men."

"So I have happy
news for you.
You will grow two sets!
Set one. Set two."

"You will lose
set number one.
And when you do,
it's not much fun.

"But then you'll grow
set number two!
32 teeth, and all brand-new.
16 downstairs, and 16 more
upstairs on the upper floor.

"And when you get your second set,
THAT'S ALL THE TEETH
YOU'LL EVER GET!"

SO . . .
don't chew down trees
like beavers do.
If you try,
you'll lose set
number two!

And . . .
don't be dumb
like Mr. Glotz.
Don't break your teeth
untying knots!

And don't be dumb
like Katy Klopps.
Don't try to chew off
bottle tops!

Don't gobble junk
like Billy Billings.
They say his teeth
have fifty fillings!

They sure are handy
when you smile.
So keep your teeth
around awhile.

And <u>never</u> bite your dentist
when he works inside your head.
Your dentist is
your teeth's best friend.

Bite someone else instead!

The KNEE BOOK

By Graham Tether

Illustrated by Sylvie Wickstrom

KNEES!

KNEES!
They're everywhere!

We see them
here.

We see them
there—

at the circus . . .

at the fair.

We need our knees,
without a doubt!

We need our knees
to walk about . . .

to jump
up high

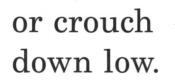

or crouch
down low.

Nothing works like knees,
you know.

Knees are great
for summer hikes . . .

for jumping rope

and riding bikes.

They help us ski.

They help us skate.

KNEES!

KNEES!

Knees are great!

While upside down
on a flying trapeze,

we'd fall on our heads
without our knees!

We use them each
and every day—

to skip,

to run . . .

to dance,

to play . . .

to mow the lawn,

to pitch the hay.

In summer, when
the weather's hot,

our knees are in
the sun a lot.

When winter comes
and the weather gets breezy,

COVER YOUR KNEES
so they don't get freezy!

So many different
kinds of knees!

Some are fat

and some are thin.

Some bend out

and some bend in . . .

and some are covered
with very thick skin.

Knees are prone
to cuts and scrapes . . .

except if you're one
of those hairy apes!

It's important to remember,
whatever you do,
that knees always come
in sets of two.

Like the wings of a bird
that flies through the air,
knees come together,
two to a pair.

Do fish have knees?
No, none at all . . .

whether they're big
or whether they're small.

No knees on sharks.

No knees on whales.

No knees on dolphins,

worms,

or snails.

If you have knees,
then you're in luck.
Without our knees,
we'd all be stuck!

For every little
move we'd make,
we'd need to slither
like a snake!

I say it once.
I say it twice.
Knees, knees are very nice!

Knees are great
in every way.

Hooray for knees!
Hip, hip, hooray!

Don't take them for granted.
Take good care of them,
please.

And always remember . . .

ENJOY YOUR KNEES!

Bright & Early Books

BEARS IN THE NIGHT by Stan and Jan Berenstain

THE BERENSTAIN BEARS AND THE SPOOKY OLD TREE
by Stan and Jan Berenstain

BLUE TRAIN, GREEN TRAIN by the Rev. W. Awdry

THE EAR BOOK by Al Perkins

THE EYE BOOK by Dr. Seuss, writing as Theo. LeSieg

FAST TRAIN, SLOW TRAIN by the Rev. W. Awdry

THE FOOT BOOK by Dr. Seuss

GREAT DAY FOR UP by Dr. Seuss

HAND, HAND, FINGERS, THUMB by Al Perkins

HOOPER HUMPERDINK . . . ? NOT HIM!
by Dr. Seuss, writing as Theo. LeSieg

I'LL TEACH MY DOG 100 WORDS by Michael Frith

IN A PEOPLE HOUSE by Dr. Seuss, writing as Theo. LeSieg

INSIDE, OUTSIDE, UPSIDE DOWN by Stan and Jan Berenstain

MARVIN K. MOONEY, WILL YOU PLEASE GO NOW!
by Dr. Seuss

MONEY, MONEY, HONEY BUNNY! by Marilyn Sadler

MR. BROWN CAN MOO! CAN YOU? by Dr. Seuss

OLD HAT, NEW HAT by Stan and Jan Berenstain

THE SHAPE OF ME AND OTHER STUFF by Dr. Seuss

THERE'S A WOCKET IN MY POCKET! by Dr. Seuss

THE TOOTH BOOK by Dr. Seuss, writing as Theo. LeSieg

WOULD YOU RATHER BE A BULLFROG?
by Dr. Seuss, writing as Theo. LeSieg

Beginner Books

ARE YOU MY MOTHER? by P. D. Eastman

THE BEARS' PICNIC by Stan and Jan Berenstain

THE BEARS' VACATION by Stan and Jan Berenstain

BECAUSE A LITTLE BUG WENT KA-CHOO! by Rosetta Stone

THE BELLY BOOK by Joe Harris

THE BERENSTAIN BEARS AND THE MISSING DINOSAUR BONE
by Stan and Jan Berenstain

THE BEST NEST by P. D. Eastman

BIG DOG . . . LITTLE DOG by P. D. Eastman

THE BIG HONEY HUNT by Stan and Jan Berenstain

THE BIKE LESSON by Stan and Jan Berenstain

CAN YOU TELL ME HOW TO GET TO SESAME STREET?
by Eleanor Hudson

THE CAT IN THE HAT by Dr. Seuss

THE CAT IN THE HAT COMES BACK by Dr. Seuss

THE CAT'S QUIZZER by Dr. Seuss

A CRACK IN THE TRACK by the Rev. W. Awdry

THE DIGGING-EST DOG by Al Perkins

DR. SEUSS'S ABC by Dr. Seuss

A FISH OUT OF WATER by Helen Palmer

FLAP YOUR WINGS by P. D. Eastman

A FLY WENT BY by Mike McClintock

FOX IN SOCKS by Dr. Seuss

FRED AND TED GO CAMPING by Peter Eastman

FRED AND TED LIKE TO FLY by Peter Eastman

FRED AND TED'S ROAD TRIP by Peter Eastman

GO, DOG. GO! by P. D. Eastman

GO, TRAIN, GO! by the Rev. W. Awdry

GREEN EGGS AND HAM by Dr. Seuss

HAVE YOU SEEN MY DINOSAUR? by Jon Surgal

HONEY BUNNY FUNNYBUNNY by Marilyn Sadler

HOP ON POP by Dr. Seuss

I AM NOT GOING TO GET UP TODAY! by Dr. Seuss

I CAN READ WITH MY EYES SHUT! by Dr. Seuss

I WANT TO BE SOMEBODY NEW! by Robert Lopshire

I WISH THAT I HAD DUCK FEET
by Dr. Seuss, writing as Theo. LeSieg

IT'S NOT EASY BEING A BUNNY by Marilyn Sadler

MRS. WOW NEVER WANTED A COW by Martha Freeman

OH SAY CAN YOU SAY? by Dr. Seuss

OH, THE THINKS YOU CAN THINK! by Dr. Seuss

ONE FISH TWO FISH RED FISH BLUE FISH by Dr. Seuss

PLEASE TRY TO REMEMBER THE FIRST OF OCTEMBER!
by Dr. Seuss, writing as Theo. LeSieg

PUT ME IN THE ZOO by Robert Lopshire

RIDDLES AND MORE RIDDLES! by Bennett Cerf

ROBERT THE ROSE HORSE by Joan Heilbroner

SAM AND THE FIREFLY by P. D. Eastman

SNOW by Roy McKie and P. D. Eastman

STOP, TRAIN, STOP! by the Rev. W. Awdry

SUMMER by Alice Low

TEN APPLES UP ON TOP! by Dr. Seuss, writing as Theo. LeSieg

TRAINS, CRANES & TROUBLESOME TRUCKS
by the Rev. W. Awdry

WACKY WEDNESDAY by Dr. Seuss, writing as Theo. LeSieg